Are We There Yet?

CTW
SESAME STREET

P9-DEW-067

A Random House PICTUREBACK® Shape Book

By Sarah Albee • Illustrated by Tom Brannon

CTW Books

Library of Congress Catalog Card Number: 99-61334 ISBN: 0-375-80436-6

www.randomhouse.com/ctwbooks www.sesamestreet.com

Printed in the United States of America January 2000 10 9 8 7 6 5 4 3 2 1

"Hurray!" cried Zoe as she clambered into her seat. "We're going for a car ride!" *Click!* went her seatbelt. *Vrooom!* went the engine.

"Here we go!" yelled Zoe.

In the city, she read the signs.

Soon they were in the country.
"A cow!" yelled Zoe excitedly. "Ooooh! Look over there!
I see sheep!"

The car went up, up, up a hill.

The car went down, down, down again.
"Wheeeeee!" shouted Zoe. "Driving in a car is fun!"

Zoe waved to the truck drivers. Some of them tooted back.

Next they stopped for gas. Zoe got to help.

Then she helped wash the windows.

Soon they were back on the road.
"We're probably almost there," said Zoe.
She checked the map.
They still had a long way to go.

"Look," said Zoe with a yawn. "Another barn."
She tried to scratch her back where it itched, but she couldn't reach.

She looked through her stacks of books.
"Read 'em all," she said.
She looked at her puzzles.
"Done 'em all," she said.
She looked at her music tapes.
"Heard 'em all," she said with a sigh.

"Guess I'll have another cracker," Zoe said. She'd already eaten a lot.

"I'll take tiny bites. Maybe by the time I finish it, we'll be there."

It didn't work.

SPEED
LIMIT
55

Zoe picked up her juice box and accidentally
squirted it all over her fur. She felt sticky. And her
tummy felt funny.

Mile after mile the car drove. Zoe couldn't stand it one minute longer.

"I am BORED, BORED, BORED!" she bellowed when they stopped at a toll booth. "Are we THERE yet?"

"Almost, dear," said her mother. "Now please sit down so I can buckle your seatbelt."

A few minutes later, the car turned off a road into a big parking lot.

"We're HERE!" shouted Zoe. "Hurray! I can't wait to get out of this car!"

"I thought we'd never get here!" she said to herself as she climbed onto her favorite ride. "Wheeeeee!"